Belinda stared at the water beyond the weeds. It looked dark and spooky.

She wondered whose spirits were lurking there, just waiting to break free.

"Strange things have been happening around the neighborhood," Miss Foster said. "Weird sounds. Lights switching off and on. Doors slamming shut. Mr. Jamison's old dog, Gomer, howling at nothing until he's hoarse..."

A chill ran across Belinda's shoulders.

The ghost of Spirit Lake

The ghost of Spirit Lake

by **Susan Saunders**
illustrated by **Jane Manning**

Harper Trophy®
A Division of HarperCollins Publishers

To Stacy Martz

Harper Trophy® is a registered trademark of
HarperCollins Publishers Inc.

The Ghost of Spirit Lake
Text copyright © 1997 by Susan Saunders
Illustrations copyright © 1997 by Jane Manning
Library of Congress Cataloging-in-Publication Data
Saunders, Susan.
     The ghost of Spirit Lake / by Susan Saunders ; illustrated by Jane Manning.
        p.   cm.   — (The Black Cat Club ; #4)
     Summary: The unfriendly ghost of Spirit Lake has a score to settle with Alice,
the Black Cat Club's ghostly member.
     ISBN 0-06-442064-7 (pbk.)
     [1. Ghosts—Fiction.]   I. Manning, Jane K., ill.   II. Title.   III. Series:
Saunders, Susan. Black Cat Club ; #4.
PZ7.S2577Gf   1997   96-49080
[Fic]—dc21   CIP
                                                                              AC

1   2   3   4   5   6   7   8   9   10
❖
First Edition

Don't miss these other Black Cat Club books:

Chapter One

"Hey, Belinda, hurry up!" "Yeah, step on it!" the impatient voices called from Belinda's living room.

"I'm coming—just give me a second!" Belinda Marks yelled from upstairs.

She was moving a lot more slowly than usual.

"Not getting enough sleep will do that to you," Belinda muttered to herself.

She finished buckling her overall straps and ran down the stairs. The Black Cat Club was going to Spirit Lake to do some exploring, and she was late.

The Black Cat Club had four members. Four members who were regular kids, anyway: Belinda, her little brother,

Andrew, Robert Sullivan, and Sam Quirk.

Sam was Belinda's next-door neighbor. He'd started the club that summer to hunt down ghosts in Maplewood.

At the time, Belinda wasn't certain that there *were* any ghosts in Maplewood. But she wasn't certain that there weren't any, either.

She didn't have to wait long to find out for sure.

Almost as soon as they started the Black Cat Club, they ran into Alice Foster at the Maplewood Free Library.

Alice Foster was most definitely a ghost. She could slip through walls and appear in the most unexpected places.

Sometimes Alice acted a lot like Andrew.

Like Andrew, Alice was seven years old—give or take a hundred years. Like Andrew, Alice wanted to have fun, play tricks on people, and hang around with other kids. Like Andrew, Alice could be a big baby. She'd get angry if anyone said "no" to her.

But *not* like Andrew, Alice could be very scary.

She was amazingly strong and could bounce large pieces of furniture around like soccer balls.

If Alice got angry enough, she could even spin herself into a fierce whirlwind.

After all, she *was* a ghost.

Once she'd left the Maplewood Free Library behind, Alice turned her attention to the Black Cat Club. She had helped them get out of trouble more than once. In fact, she became sort of a fifth member of the club.

She'd pop in on one or another of the kids whenever she felt like it—usually in the middle of the night.

Belinda would be sleeping peacefully in her room.

All of a sudden, the covers would fly off her bed.

What happened next depended on

Alice's mood. Icy fingers might brush past Belinda's ear. A frosty breeze might freeze the tip of her nose.

Then a ghostly bell would jingle.

And there would be a strong smell of chocolate in the air. Alice loved chocolate.

Belinda, Robert, and Sam had seen her just once. Only Andrew could see Alice most of the time, in her long white dress and high-top shoes. Maybe it was because they were exactly the same age.

Sometimes Belinda saw what looked like whitish smoke.

Other times she could see only what Alice was doing.

And Alice did plenty.

She'd jerk open the closet door and toss Belinda's clothes around.

Or she would dig through the basket where Belinda kept her cassette tapes. Alice would pop one into the tape player. She'd turn the volume up as high as it would go.

Belinda's mom and dad weren't exactly thrilled about loud music at three o'clock in the morning.

"What has gotten into you, Belinda?" Mr. Marks had asked his daughter just the night before. "I don't mind rock music. But not when it's blasting in the middle of the night!"

"And look at the mess you've made of your closet," Mrs. Marks added, shaking her head.

What was Belinda supposed to tell her parents: "I didn't do it—my ghost friend Alice did"?

Instead Belinda mumbled, "Sorry—I must have been sleepwalking."

"I wish *I* were!" said her father. "Unfortunately, I'm wide awake."

Thankfully, Alice disappeared right after that.

Belinda often wondered where Alice went when she wasn't bugging them.

Did ghosts ever rest?

And just where was Alice now?

Belinda's black cat, Mittens, was

sound asleep on the desk chair. That usually meant Alice was nowhere near. When she was, Mittens made himself scarce.

"Alice," Belinda said in a low voice. "Alice, are you still here?" Then she added, "You'd better be somewhere close."

After all, the main reason Belinda was going to the lake today was for Alice.

She wanted to find Alice a friend.

A girl ghost, about Alice's age, without much to do . . .

Belinda wasn't sure that the others would go along with her plan.

Andrew liked having a ghost around, especially one just his age.

Sam thought Alice was cool too. And she proved that the Black Cat Club was a great idea.

Not Robert. Alice had scared Robert half to death a few times. He probably wouldn't be interested in finding another ghost for Alice to be friends with, either. He just wanted her to disappear permanently.

But Belinda hoped they'd get lucky that day at Spirit Lake. She hoped they'd find a nice ghost for Alice to hang out with. Then Alice wouldn't be lonely.

And then maybe Alice would give the Black Cat Club a break!

Chapter Two

Sam, Belinda, Robert, and Andrew pedaled their bikes down Grove Lane, on their way to Spirit Lake.

"What makes you think there are ghosts at the lake, anyway?" Robert asked Sam.

"It's called *Spirit* Lake," Sam said. "And *spirit* is just another word for *ghost,* right?"

"Not that I care—I'm only going to the lake to fish," Robert said quickly.

He figured they already had one ghost too many!

"Whose ghosts are in the lake?" Andrew wanted to know.

"Well, they say it's haunted by

the spirits of people who drowned," said Sam.

"Who says so?" Andrew asked.

"The old-timers around Maplewood say so," Sam told him.

"Andrew, stop asking so many questions," Belinda said crossly.

She glanced over her shoulder. She was looking for those wisps of whitish smoke. . . .

If Belinda *hadn't* wanted Alice to follow her that day, she could never have gotten rid of her.

Since Belinda *did* want Alice around, she probably would never show up.

Hopefully, Belinda sniffed the air for the smell of chocolate.

What she smelled was a lot more like dead fish than candy.

"Yuck!" Belinda said. "What stinks?"

"I guess it's the lake," said Sam. "But I don't remember it ever smelling this bad."

They turned off Grove Lane.

They bumped along the dirt road

leading to the picnic area.

The smell grew even stronger.

"It's like the bottom of a swamp," said Belinda, wrinkling her nose.

"The smellier, the better. Maybe it'll keep Alice away from us. Like the garlic did that time," Robert said.

"Well, it's definitely keeping *other* people away," said Belinda.

In the summer, the picnic grounds beside Spirit Lake were always crowded with people. That day, there was no one in sight.

"Great—I'll have the fish all to myself," said Robert. "There's the fishing shack."

He pointed to a small wooden hut beyond the picnic tables.

The painted sign on the front said JOE-BOB'S BAIT. RED WIGGLERS. I RENT FISHING POLES TOO.

"You guys can hunt for ghosts if you want," Robert said. "I'm renting a pole."

He braked in front of the fishing shack. "Just call me when you're done," he added.

"I want to see the spirits," Andrew murmured, steering his bike around the side of the shack.

Suddenly he called out. "Hey—there's no water!"

"What is he talking about?" asked his sister.

Belinda, Sam, and Robert rode their bikes around the side of the shack too.

Usually Spirit Lake lapped right up against the back of the fishing shack.

Now tall weeds grew where the water used to be—tall weeds and greenish slime.

"*P-U*," said Andrew, holding his nose.

An older man peered out the back window of the shack. JOE-BOB was printed on the front of his cap.

"The water's out there somewhere," Joe-Bob said. "Way past the weeds. The lake has never been this low before."

"The lake's drying up?" said Sam.

"How could it be? It's been raining all summer," said Belinda.

"Not raining enough," said Joe-Bob.

"People are watering their yards. And their farms. More water goes out of the lake than gets rained back into it. And the river isn't feeding the lake either. Parts of Forge River are bone-dry."

"Can I still fish?" Robert asked him.

"You bet," said Joe-Bob. "You'll just have to walk a ways. There may be less water in the lake, but there are just as many fish. That adds up to a lot more fish per square inch."

"What about the spirits?" asked Andrew. "Are there more spirits per square inch too?"

Joe-Bob laughed. "I haven't seen any spirits myself," he said. "But you could talk to that lady over there. She was telling me about some strange happenings that have been going on."

Not far away, a woman stood on a flat rock and gazed out at the shrunken lake. She was very small and a little stooped. She had snow-white hair.

"We know her!" said Andrew.

"That's Miss Foster," said Belinda.

"Strange happenings?" Sam repeated.

"Here we go again," said Robert with a sigh.

Chapter Three

The Black Cat Club had first met Miss Foster when they were trying to find out about Alice.

Miss Foster was Alice's youngest sister.

But she had never known Alice. Miss Foster was born a few years after Alice died of a fever in 1899.

Miss Foster had shown the kids pictures of the whole Foster family. And she told them some things her brother had told her about her departed sister.

Like how much Alice loved chocolate.

And how the Foster children used to

leave chocolate candy out for Alice long after she'd died.

Miss Foster said she was never sure if Alice's ghost *did* visit them at night, or if it was one of her brothers or sisters who took the candy.

The Black Cat Club didn't tell Miss Foster that Alice's ghost was very real. They hadn't wanted to give her an awful shock, not at her age.

Now had Miss Foster found a spirit on her own?

"Maybe she'd like to talk about it," said Sam, propping his bike against the fishing shack.

"I'll go with you," said Belinda.

"I'm going too," said Andrew.

"I'm going fishing," Robert said firmly.

Belinda, Sam, and Andrew left Robert at the fishing shack and hurried toward Miss Foster.

"Is Miss Foster an old-timer?" Andrew asked as they picked their way across the sticky mud.

"I don't know anybody older," said Sam.

When they walked out onto the rock, Andrew said, "Are there really spirits in Spirit Lake, Miss Foster? Sam says you're old enough to know."

"Andrew!" exclaimed his sister.

"Why, you're the children who asked me about my sister Alice," Miss Foster said.

Sam, Belinda, and Andrew nodded.

Belinda stared at the water beyond the weeds. It looked dark and spooky.

She wondered whose spirits were lurking there, just waiting to break free.

"Strange things have been happening around the neighborhood," Miss Foster said. "Weird sounds. Lights switching off and on. Doors slamming shut. Mr. Jamison's old dog, Gomer, howling at nothing until he's hoarse . . ."

A chill ran across Belinda's shoulders.

"I've been feeling uneasy myself," Miss Foster said. "Then, last night, something *really* strange happened."

Belinda swallowed hard.

"It was almost midnight," said Miss Foster. "I thought I heard a knock at my living room window. My cat sometimes taps with her paw to be let in."

Miss Foster went on, "I walked downstairs to the living room. I saw something moving just outside the window. It kind of looked like a person—a very *lumpy* person. I switched on the porch light. The . . . whatever it was . . . slipped away, through the trees. It was heading toward the lake."

"Where's your house?" Andrew asked her.

The Black Cat Club had only seen Miss Foster's house from the front.

"That's my back fence, over there," Miss Foster told them, pointing over her shoulder.

The fence wasn't more than thirty yards away.

If spirits really were leaving the lake, they didn't have all that far to go to get to Miss Foster's. . . .

"Then I turned on the lights in the living room," Miss Foster said. "The window closest to my glass-front cabinet had been raised a few inches. The cabinet door was open. And something was missing from the top shelf."

"Wh-what?" Belinda asked, breathlessly.

"A silver compass," said Miss Foster. "It isn't worth anything. That is to say, it isn't worth much money. But it's the only thing I have that belonged to my sister Alice."

"So the compass must be a hundred years old!" Andrew said.

"Older than that," Miss Foster replied. "It belonged to my grandfather first. His name was Adam Foster, and he gave it to Alice because they had the same initials: *AF*."

Belinda was busy working out the possibilities: *Could Alice have taken the compass herself?* she wondered.

Belinda's answer was, *She probably did!*

Alice hadn't turned on Belinda's tape player until three o'clock that morning. Which gave her plenty of time to take the compass out of Miss Foster's cabinet at midnight.

Maybe when Alice wasn't driving the Black Cat Club crazy, she was causing trouble elsewhere in Maplewood. Like at her own sister's house!

Miss Foster went on, "The oddest thing . . . the bottom of the window, a corner of my carpet, and one of the handles of the glass cabinet were streaked with dark, smelly mud."

But Alice doesn't seem like the mud-pie type, Belinda thought.

Belinda recalled the one time she'd really been able to see Alice. The ghost wore a spotless white dress and neatly polished black shoes. . . .

On the other hand, who would be more likely to want Alice's compass than Alice?

And maybe she'd smeared herself with mud from the lake to look scary.

Alice enjoyed scaring people.

"Have you cleaned up the mud already?" Sam asked Miss Foster.

"Not yet—I wanted to try to make some sense of it first," said Miss Foster. She added, "Would you be interested in taking a look?"

"Sure," said Sam.

Belinda knew Sam would like nothing better.

"Shouldn't we yell for Robert?" Andrew asked.

Belinda peered toward Joe-Bob's fishing shack, then out past the mud and the weeds.

She could just make out Robert's green shirt at the edge of the murky water.

"Robert's fishing," Belinda said.

"We'll come back for him later," said Sam.

The three of them followed Miss Foster to her house. It was time to examine the evidence.

Chapter Four

Miss Foster lived in a small, two-story house covered with ivy. A stone path led from the back gate to the kitchen door. Then the path curved around the house, past the living room windows.

"Stop!" Sam said before they set foot on the stone path. "Miss Foster, is there mud on these stones?"

"How smart of you!" said Miss Foster. "I didn't think to look."

While Belinda, Andrew, and Miss Foster waited just outside the gate, Sam got down on his hands and knees. He stared at the stone path.

"No mud," Sam said. "So whatever it was, it didn't walk on this path."

Alice doesn't have to walk at all, Belinda was thinking. *She floats.*

And her next thought was, *Alice, I bet you're watching all of this and laughing your head off.*

"Let's go inside," said Miss Foster.

She opened the back door to her house.

Before they followed Miss Foster into her kitchen, Belinda whispered to Andrew, "Is Alice near? Can you see her?"

Andrew glanced around the yard, then shook his head.

"Nope," he said. "No Alice."

Sam mumbled, "There's something spooky going on, though...." He stopped himself.

"And just how do you know that?" Belinda said.

She knew Sam couldn't see Alice either.

So he was just showing off.

"Shhh. Later," Sam whispered.

He looked sorry he'd said anything.

"Right through here, into the living room," said Miss Foster.

The kids passed the small table crowded with Foster family photographs. There was the picture they'd already seen of Alice, on the farm with her mom and dad and brothers and sisters.

Miss Foster pointed to her sister's photo. "If you look closely, you can see the silver compass. She wore it pinned to the front of her dress."

In the photograph, Alice wore the compass proudly, a big smile on her face.

As cross as she was with Alice, the picture made Belinda sad.

Alice looked so happy. She hadn't known that soon she would be leaving her family forever.

"I'll raise the window as I found it," said Miss Foster, crossing the living room.

She lifted the window closest to the glass cabinet four or five inches.

"It won't go any higher—it jams," Miss Foster explained.

"Not much more than a hand fits through," Sam said, trying it.

But what about a ghost? Belinda was thinking. *Alice can slide under doors and slip through keyholes.*

"There's some mud on it," Miss Foster said.

She pointed to the bottom of the window.

"And on the carpet . . . and here," said Sam. He stared closely at the handle of the glass cabinet.

"There's a bit of dried mud inside the

cabinet, too," said Miss Foster. "Right where I kept Alice's silver compass."

"Hey!" a voice called from the back door. "Are you guys in there?"

"It's our friend Robert," Belinda said to Miss Foster.

"Please come in," Miss Foster called to him.

Robert hurried into the room, tracking more mud onto the rug.

In his left hand he held a fishing pole. Robert's right hand completely covered whatever was hanging from the fish hook.

"Guess what I caught?" asked Robert.

"A really small fish?" Andrew said.

"Way cooler than that," said Robert. He opened his right hand.

The kids saw a clump of green water weed.

"You caught lake slime," said Sam.

"No. *Look*," Robert said.

He handed the fishing pole to Belinda.

Then Robert lifted the weeds. Something shiny and silver was caught on the fish hook.

"I'm not sure what it is, but it looks really old," Robert said.

"Maybe it belongs to one of the spirits," said Andrew.

But there was a cry of surprise from Miss Foster. "I believe it's . . ."

Miss Foster reached over and slipped the shiny object off the fish hook. She held it up to the light from the window.

"It is!" Miss Foster cried. "It's Alice's compass!"

Chapter Five

The compass case was solid silver. The initials *A* and *F* were carved into the front of it, twined together.

Miss Foster showed the kids how to open the case.

"You push in this little button on the top," she said.

The front of the case flipped down. Inside, glass covered the face of the compass. A tiny steel needle swung around to point north.

"Cool!" said Andrew.

"I almost can't believe this!" Miss Foster said. "The compass disappeared from the cabinet just last night. And not much more than twelve hours later, you were lucky enough to fish it out of Spirit Lake."

Sam wasn't listening. He was peering through the living room window, glancing around Miss Foster's yard.

Who is Sam looking for? Belinda wondered. *Alice, maybe?*

Belinda stared out the window too.

"Now it's near the trees . . ." Sam was mumbling.

Belinda thought she saw something in the shadow of the pines.

Was it an animal? A person? Or just a tree?

Then it moved.

Didn't it?

Belinda rubbed her eyes hard.

She squinted out the living room window again.

All she saw were pine trees. And a rotting tree stump.

"I can't thank you enough for bringing this back to me," Miss Foster was saying.

"Would you like some cookies and

milk? Or strawberry ice cream?" she added.

"Sure!" said Andrew. He was always ready for a snack. "Okay, Belinda?"

"No, thank you," Sam said quickly to Miss Foster. "We really have to get going."

And he started toward the back door.

"Sam, could you hang on one second?" said Belinda.

There was a favor Belinda wanted to ask of Miss Foster. She'd wanted to ease into it, but now there wasn't time.

So Belinda blurted it out. "Miss Foster, could I borrow the compass? Just overnight?"

"Well . . . I suppose you . . ." Miss Foster began.

"My dad would just love to take a look at it," Belinda added.

It was a tiny lie.

Miss Foster nodded. "Of course you can take it. If it weren't for you children, I wouldn't have it back at all," she said.

Miss Foster handed the compass to Belinda.

It was heavy, and cool to the touch.

Belinda thought of how happy Alice looked in the photo with the shiny compass pinned to the front of her dress.

It wasn't hard to understand why Alice had slipped through the window. Or why she'd popped open Miss Foster's glass cabinet to take the compass.

But she had made a mess—and upset her sister.

And why had Alice thrown the compass into Spirit Lake?

Maybe if Alice couldn't use the compass, she didn't want anyone else to enjoy it either. Not even her own sister.

Alice could be such a brat!

"I'll bring the compass back first thing tomorrow morning," Belinda promised Miss Foster.

She buttoned it carefully into the chest pocket of her overalls.

Belinda wanted the compass as proof.

She planned to give Alice a serious talking-to when she visited Belinda's room that night.

It was bad enough when Alice was driving the Black Cat Club bananas.

But now she was running all over town, frightening old ladies.

It had to stop!

Chapter Six

By the time Belinda, Andrew, and Robert said good-bye to Miss Foster at her kitchen door, Sam was halfway to the back gate.

"Sam, why are you in such a hurry?" Robert asked when they caught up with him.

"Yeah, and why are you acting so weird?" Belinda asked. "Did you see a *ghost*?" she added with a nervous laugh.

But Sam was serious—dead serious. "I don't *see* ghosts. I *hear* them," he said.

Sam didn't slow down. He marched straight across the mud toward the flat rock where Miss Foster had been standing.

"We can all *hear* them," said Robert. "Alice's stupid bell jingling . . ."

"And smell them, too," said Belinda. "Alice has totally ruined chocolate for me. I can't unwrap a candy bar without thinking that she's—"

Sam interrupted Belinda.

"No, I'm not talking about hearing Alice's bell," he said. "I'm talking about . . ."

Sam thought for a moment about how to explain himself.

Finally he said, "I hear it inside my head. It's like buzzing, or crackling. Like static."

"Maybe you just need to wash out your ears," Andrew said helpfully.

Sam stopped short and glared at all three of them. "Will you guys please listen to what I'm saying?"

He began again.

"If there aren't any ghosts around, I don't hear anything," Sam said. "But as soon as there's a ghost anywhere near me, the crackling starts. The closer the ghost gets, the louder the noise gets inside my head."

"It's sort of like a smoke alarm. Only it's a ghost alarm!" said Andrew.

"Right!" said Sam.

"Prove it," said Robert.

Robert didn't believe a word Sam was saying.

Belinda was having a hard time believing Sam too.

"How can I prove it?" said Sam. "I first noticed it at the library, with Alice. I always knew when she was hanging around."

"Oh sure," said Robert. "So how come you never told us about it?"

"Because I knew you wouldn't believe me!" said Sam. "Plus I had trouble believing it myself."

Sam went on, "But the same thing happened with the next ghost—Rad Man. The buzzing started as soon as we found that old skateboard. And the cat mummy at the museum made my radar buzz like two dozen electric drills!"

"'Radar'?" said Belinda.

"That's what I call it," Sam said. *"Ghost radar."*

Robert snorted.

"You can believe it or not," Sam said. "But I just heard it loud and clear at Miss Foster's."

He started walking again, fast.

"And the closer we get to Spirit Lake, the more noise my radar makes," he added.

Sam stepped onto the flat rock and stared out at the dark lake.

"In fact, my radar's never buzzed any louder than it's buzzing right now," he said.

A chill ran up Belinda's spine.

But she said, "It's probably just Alice. She likes to get us going. And who else would have had a reason to take the compass?"

Belinda stepped onto the rock, too, and glanced around. She was hoping to spot some whitish smoke.

Suddenly Robert said, "Who was that strange kid at Miss Foster's?"

"What strange kid?" Belinda asked.

"The kid in the backyard. I said 'hi' to him, but he disappeared behind a tree," Robert answered.

Goosebumps ran down Belinda's arms.

Was that who she'd seen through Miss Foster's window?

Sam stopped staring at the lake and stared at Robert.

"What did the kid look like?" Sam asked.

"I couldn't really see him very well," said Robert. "He was built kind of . . . stocky. And lumpy."

"Lumpy?" Belinda and Sam said at the same time.

That was exactly the same word Miss Foster had used about the odd figure she'd seen the night before.

And it sounded pretty much like what Belinda had just seen herself!

"It seemed like a kid to you?" Sam asked Robert.

"It *was* a kid," Robert said. "Wasn't it?"

Robert cracked his knuckles, the way he did when he was getting spooked.

"A kid can't turn up my radar like this. And neither can Alice," Sam said.

Belinda was getting a creepy feeling.

What if Sam's radar was right?

What if there *was* something out there in the shrinking lake? Breaking free of the shallow water whenever it wanted . . .

What about that lumpy creature wandering around Miss Foster's neighborhood?

It's one of Alice's tricks, Belinda said firmly to herself.

Still . . .

"Uh . . . I told my dad I'd mow the lawn this afternoon," Robert was saying. He turned away from Spirit Lake, cracking his knuckles again. "I'd better return this fishing pole and go home."

So Belinda said, "Andrew and I have to leave too. I told Mom we'd . . . go shopping with her."

"Why'd you do that?" said Andrew. "I hate shopping."

"We're going, and that's final," Belinda said to her little brother.

"We can always come back tomorrow," said Sam. "The spirits will still be here."

Unless they're out wandering around town, Belinda said to herself.

Robert turned in his pole at the fishing shack.

The four kids got on their bikes and headed toward their houses on Mill Lane.

The ride home was a quiet one.

Belinda had a lot to think about.

Was Alice just playing a dumb trick on them? If not, who, or *what*, was this lumpy creature? And what did it want?

Belinda didn't have a clue.

There was one thing Belinda *did*

know: She was glad to leave Spirit Lake behind.

She liked it a lot better when it was filled to the brim!

Chapter Seven

Belinda put the silver compass on her bedside table, right next to the alarm clock. When Alice showed up in the middle of the night, Belinda would be ready for her!

Once she'd crawled into bed that evening, Belinda practiced what she was going to say. "Alice, you've really been acting like a brat. For one thing, you're getting me in trouble with my parents. Plus I need my sleep. For another, you can't go around scaring old ladies and stealing things out of their houses."

Okay, maybe it wasn't *really* stealing. The compass had belonged to Alice in the first place. And to her grandfather before that.

Still, Miss Foster loved having that compass. Alice didn't have any right to throw it away. . . .

Belinda dozed off.

She wasn't sure just what woke her up.

Maybe it was Mittens.

The black cat was pressing himself tightly against her back. She could feel him shivering.

"Alice?" Belinda whispered.

She heard Alice's bell jingle a few times.

"We found your compass in Spirit Lake," Belinda muttered. "Why did you take it from Miss Foster if you were just going to throw it away?"

The bell stopped for a moment.

"Your own sister, Alice," Belinda went on. "How could you be so mean?"

The bell started ringing again, very fast.

"It's no use getting mad at me,"

Belinda whispered. "You knew she was your sister, and you—"

The bell rang even faster and louder.

"You *did* know she was your sister, right?" said Belinda. "Miss Foster, on the lake?"

Maybe Alice hadn't known!

Miss Foster was born after Alice died, after all.

But before Belinda could find out for sure, a strong smell suddenly filled the room.

It sure wasn't chocolate.

It was a terrible, damp, swampy, dead-fishy smell, and Belinda had smelled it before.

For a split second, Belinda thought Alice had somehow whisked her to the shore of Spirit Lake. As a joke, maybe.

But no, there was the alarm clock on her bedside table. The glowing numbers said *12:10*—it was just after midnight.

Was the silver compass still on the table too?

Belinda reached out for it.

Her hand hit a patch of freezing-cold air right beside her bed.

Belinda jerked her hand back, and sucked in her breath.

She nearly gagged. That awful smell was even stronger!

"Alice . . . ?" Belinda said softly.

Suddenly the bell was drowned out by shrill, crazy giggling.

That wasn't Alice!

There was an angry shriek.

That *was* Alice!

Still the crazy giggling went on and on.

Belinda was filled with a terrible feeling of dread.

Maybe Alice needed her help.

But Belinda had to get away from that horrible giggling!

She tugged the covers over her head.

She burrowed under her pillow and made herself count to two hundred.

Then, slowly, she pulled her head out from under the pillow.

All was quiet in her bedroom.

The crazy giggling had stopped.

Alice's bell wasn't ringing any longer.

And the lake smell was gone too.

Mittens was still pressed against her back. He was stiff with fright.

"I'm turning on the light," Belinda said softly.

She made herself reach out from under the covers.

No cold spot.

She switched on the lamp beside her bed.

Her window was wide open.

Even from her bed, she could see that the sill was streaked with mud.

Belinda peered over the edge of the bed, to the floor.

A trail of mud led from the window, across the rug, to her bedside.

There was a blob of mud on the table: a blob of mud, and no silver compass.

She jumped out of bed and ran to the window.

A brownish, lumpy figure was moving through the light cast by the streetlight.

It seemed to be dragging something along with it, something that didn't want to go.

Or someone . . .

"Alice?" Belinda called as loudly as she dared.

There was another angry shriek.

Then the lumpy figure lurched out of the light and disappeared into the darkness.

Chapter Eight

Belinda hardly slept after that.

She tossed and turned, worrying about Alice.

When she did close her eyes, her mind replayed the sight of that creepy creature dragging Alice away.

At the first sign of light the next morning, Belinda pulled on her clothes. She slipped out of her house and hurried across the yard to the Quirks'.

Belinda looked for a pebble to throw at Sam's window to wake him up.

But Sam's voice whispered down to her, "I'll be right there."

Did Sam already know what had happened?

As soon as he stepped outside, Belinda asked, "Did you see that thing last night?"

"I *heard* him first," Sam told her. "I was sound asleep. My ghost radar started buzzing so loudly that it woke me up."

Belinda was starting to believe him.

"I thought Alice must be somewhere in my room," Sam went on. "But her bell wasn't ringing. So I looked out the window. And I spotted that . . . mud ghost."

Sam had said it: *ghost.*

"What was he doing?" said Belinda.

"He was leaning out your window," Sam said.

The hair on the back of Belinda's neck stood straight up.

"All of a sudden he floated down to the ground—two stories," Sam said. "He glided up the sidewalk, past the streetlight. That's when I saw that he wasn't alone."

"Did he have Alice with him?" Belinda asked breathlessly.

"I couldn't see *her*," Sam said. "But the mud ghost was definitely holding on to something. Something—or somebody—was fighting to pull away from him. He was getting jerked all over the place."

"I guess he's just too strong for Alice," Belinda said unhappily.

The Black Cat Club had found another ghost, all right.

And the ghost wanted to hang around with Alice, just as Belinda had hoped.

But this ghost was a monster!

Robert was crossing Mill Lane from his house.

He cracked his knuckles as he walked over to them.

"What's going on?" Robert said. "Something happened last night, didn't it?"

"How did you know?" asked Belinda.

"I thought I heard somebody yell. When I looked out my window, I saw that same weird, lumpy kid from Miss

Foster's," Robert said.

"He's not a kid—he's a ghost," said Sam. "I picked him up on my radar."

This time, Robert didn't argue about the radar.

But he did say, "He's awfully solid-looking for a ghost. You sure can't see through *him*."

"It's mud. I think he rolls in it to look bigger and scarier," Sam said.

"He pulled Alice out of my room, Robert!" Belinda said. "He took the compass, too."

"Alice is gone?" asked Robert.

Belinda couldn't tell if he was sorry or not.

"I'm always saying I'd like some time off from Alice," Belinda said to Sam and Robert. "That I'd like to find her a nice ghost to hang out with. But not this ghost."

"We'll get her back," Sam said.

"We will?" said Robert.

"We will. Think of everything she's done for us," Sam said.

"Saved you from Rad Man," Belinda pointed out to Robert.

"Saved us all from Rad Man," said Sam. "And fought the ghost of the cat mummy, too."

"Okay, okay," Robert said. "But how do we get her back? For starters, we don't even know where Alice is."

"I have a pretty good idea," Sam said.

"You do?" said Robert.

"This ghost is covered with mud, right?" said Sam.

"And he smells just like the lake," said Belinda, remembering last night's visit. "So it's lake mud."

"So that means . . . that he's taken Alice to Spirit Lake?" said Robert.

"That's what I'm guessing," Sam said.

Chapter Nine

Belinda would have left for Spirit Lake that very minute—Alice needed their help!

But Mr. Marks got up early himself.

He said Belinda and Andrew weren't going anywhere until they'd straightened up their rooms.

There were chores for Robert to do at his house, too.

Plus Sam's aunt Jennifer was staying with the Quirks, and Sam had to have breakfast with her.

So it wasn't until the middle of the morning when the Black Cat Club propped their bikes against Joe-Bob's fishing shack.

They breathed in the thick, swampy air.

"It still stinks, big-time," said Robert. "But there are a lot more people here today."

"It's Saturday," Andrew reminded him.

A man with a video camera was filming some birds.

Three guys were fishing beyond the water weeds.

There were even a couple of sunbathers lying on deck chairs.

"Anything on your radar?" Belinda asked Sam.

"Nope," said Sam. "And with all of these people around, any clues Alice might have left behind are probably gone by now," he added.

"That's Miss Foster, isn't it?" Andrew said.

She was standing near the edge of the mud, staring at something in her hand.

When the kids ran over to her, Miss Foster's face lit up.

"I'm so glad to see you," she said. "I very much wanted to phone you. But then I realized I didn't know your last names."

"Marks," said Belinda.

"Sullivan," Robert said.

"Quirk," said Sam.

"Did you want to talk to us about something, Miss Foster?" said Belinda.

Belinda knew she had to tell Miss Foster about the missing compass. And she wasn't looking forward to it.

"Yes," said Miss Foster, opening her hand. "I wanted to talk to you about this."

"Alice's compass!" said Belinda, her heart pounding. "Where did you find it?"

"Here at the lake," said Miss Foster. "I couldn't imagine you dropping it. You buttoned it into your pocket so carefully."

"It was stolen out of my room last night," said Belinda.

"Oh, dear," said Miss Foster. "What is it about this compass. . . ?"

"Can you remember exactly where you found it?" asked Sam.

Miss Foster nodded. "It was right beside those wooden posts," she told him.

The Black Cat Club walked slowly with Miss Foster, crossing the mud to reach a dozen half-buried posts.

"They were probably part of a dock at one time," Miss Foster said.

"The compass was lying at the base of this short post," she added, pointing.

Sam knelt down, searching for more clues.

"The mud looks sort of kicked up here," he said.

"Last night I dreamed about my sister Alice," Miss Foster said. "And the dream was so real.

"Alice was wearing the white dress she has on in the photograph," Miss Foster continued. "And, just as clear as that picture, I suddenly saw these wooden posts.

"So as soon as I finished breakfast, I

thought I'd better walk over here," Miss Foster said. "At the bottom of the short post, there was Alice's compass!"

Miss Foster looked at the kids and said, "It almost seemed as if Alice herself had visited me. And that she'd left the compass here for me. On purpose."

Maybe Alice did leave it on purpose, as a clue for Miss Foster! Belinda said to herself.

Belinda had heard stories about family members being able to send thoughts to each other.

She'd never been interested in trying it with Andrew.

What kind of thoughts would Andrew be having, anyway: "I'm pretending I'm Gigantor on *Wrestlemania*"?

But sharing thoughts with a ghost would be awesome!

"I just remembered something else about the dream," Miss Foster added. "Gridley was in it too. I haven't thought of him in seventy-five years or more!"

"Who's Gridley?" Robert asked her.

"He was a boy about Alice's age: Gridley Pratt," Miss Foster replied. "Only he was so terrible that everyone called him 'Gridley Bratt.' "

"Did he grow up to be nice?" Andrew wanted to know.

"He didn't grow up at all, I'm afraid," said Miss Foster. "By the time he was eleven years old, Gridley was completely wild.

"One evening he took a boat without permission. He rowed it into the middle of Spirit Lake during a fearsome thunderstorm," Miss Foster told them. "Gridley was struck by lightning. He fell out of the boat and drowned."

Wow! Andrew's mouth formed the word silently.

"I don't believe they ever found Gridley's body," said Miss Foster.

Belinda, Sam, and Robert all looked at each other.

"I think we know who dragged Alice away," Sam said quietly to the others.

"Gridley Bratt!" whispered Belinda.

Chapter Ten

The Black Cat Club knew they had to tell Miss Foster about Alice.

It was the only way they could ask for Miss Foster's help.

And they needed all the help they could get.

"You know your sister Alice . . ." Sam began.

"Yes?" Miss Foster said.

"Well, we've . . . we've met her," said Sam.

"At least, we've met her ghost," Belinda added.

"So my brother Jasper wasn't teasing!" Miss Foster exclaimed. "Alice did come to our house at night when I was a child. She did take the candy we left out for her."

The Black Cat Club nodded.

"We didn't tell you before because we didn't want to scare you," Belinda said.

"When you're my age, nothing really scares you anymore," said Miss Foster. Then she added, "Have you *seen* Alice? What's she like? How is she?"

"Andrew can see her most of the time," Belinda said.

"Right now Alice is in trouble," said Sam.

"What kind of trouble?" Miss Foster asked. She looked concerned.

"Big trouble," said Robert. "We're very worried about her."

"Alice got really excited when I told her about you last night," Belinda said to Miss Foster. "Maybe she was trying to send you a message in the dream."

"Trying to let you know where she was," said Sam.

"Stuck in Spirit Lake," Andrew said sadly.

"And letting you know who dragged her in, too," said Robert.

"It was Gridley, wasn't it!" said Miss Foster. "Because Gridley and Alice knew one another. Jasper told me about an awful fight the two of them once had."

She thought hard for a moment. "As a matter of fact, they were fighting over this very *compass*! Gridley tried to take it from Alice—he said compasses weren't for girls, only for boys. But Alice managed to hang on to it."

"Maybe Gridley never gave up on getting the compass for himself, though," said Belinda. "And neither did his ghost."

"His ghost was trapped in Spirit Lake because Gridley drowned here," said Sam.

"But now that the lake is shrinking, and the water isn't so deep . . ." said Belinda.

"His ghost got out," finished Andrew.

Robert frowned at the dark water

and cracked his knuckles.

"Gridley starting wandering around your neighborhood. He must have seen your last name on the mailbox and figured you were related to Alice. So he went into your house and found the compass," said Sam. "He stole it, and took it back to Spirit Lake. Then Robert caught it on his hook."

"Gridley came looking for the compass again. When he realized we had it, he must have followed us back to Mill Lane. He grabbed the compass. And Alice," said Belinda. "Now Alice is in Spirit Lake too. And it's our fault!"

"Alice has beaten Gridley before," Andrew said hopefully.

"She must have gotten the compass away from him last night," said Sam. "Or Miss Foster wouldn't have found it here."

"That's probably why the mud is scuffed up," Robert added.

"She may have gotten the compass, but she'll never be able to get away from Gridley." Belinda was worried.

"He's bigger than she is now. He's eleven, and she's only seven," said Andrew.

"We'll just have to give Alice some great reasons to fight a lot harder against Gridley Pratt," said Sam.

"We have to hurry," Miss Foster said suddenly. "I listened to my radio this morning. There's been a lot of rain upriver. At noon they're opening one of the dams to let some of the water drain into Spirit Lake!"

"The water in the lake will rise . . ." Sam began.

"And if we don't get Alice away from Gridley soon, she could be trapped in Spirit Lake forever!" Robert finished.

Now even Robert sounded really upset.

Chapter Eleven

We'll just have to give Alice some great reasons to fight a lot harder against Gridley Pratt, Sam had said.

What were the best reasons the Black Cat Club could think of?

"Chocolate," said Andrew.

"And you, Miss Foster," said Sam.

"That's right—you're her sister forever," said Belinda.

"We'll need a boat," said Robert.

"An old lady and four children in a boat?" said Miss Foster. "Is that a good idea?"

"I know about boats," Robert told her. He'd sailed with his uncle a few times.

And Sam said, "I don't think we have a choice if we want to get to Alice."

They all stared past the mud and water weeds at the waters of Spirit Lake.

"Alice is out there somewhere," Sam said. "Gridley is holding her down."

"I have an old rowboat of my brother's," said Miss Foster.

"Great!" said Sam.

"It hasn't been used in years," she said. "I'm not even sure it will float."

"There's no time to look around for a better one," Robert said.

"We'll row out onto the lake, just like Gridley did!" said Andrew.

"I hope not too much like Gridley," said his sister. "I'd like to be alive at the end of this!"

"We need some chocolates, too, Miss Foster," Sam reminded her.

"I have a bag of them in the kitchen. Alice isn't the only member of the family with a sweet tooth," Miss Foster said.

Miss Foster's rowboat was propped against her garage. The kids studied it as Miss Foster went inside to get the candy. The boat was wooden, with flaking paint and a mess of deep nicks and scratches.

"It looks as old as Miss Foster!" Andrew whispered.

"And leaky, too," said Belinda.

"Here's a can," said Robert, reaching under a paddle. "You can scoop out any water that leaks in."

Sam found life jackets for everyone in the garage.

"So we're all set," said Belinda, more bravely than she felt.

But it took much longer to drag the boat across the mud than they'd imagined.

"It's a lot heavier than it looks," Belinda said, huffing and puffing.

"This mud is like glue," said Sam.

Miss Foster hurried out to them with the bag of chocolates.

She tossed the bag into the rowboat and started pulling it too.

"Maybe you should let *us* get the boat into the lake," Robert said to Miss Foster.

He was worried that she might hurt herself.

But she wouldn't hear of it.

"Alice is my sister—of course I'm going to help, every step of the way!" Miss Foster said.

It must have been thoughts of Alice that made Miss Foster surprisingly strong. With her help, the Black Cat Club got the boat into the water.

"It's floating!" said Andrew, standing in Spirit Lake up to his knees.

"I'll hold the boat steady," Robert said. "Everybody get in."

"Not Andrew," said Belinda. "Mom

and Dad will kill me if anything happens to him."

"But I'm Alice's best friend!" Andrew said. "She'll come out of the lake if I'm in the boat."

"He could be right," Sam said to Belinda.

"It's not like we're all kids," Robert pointed out. "Miss Foster is a grown-up."

"And we're running out of time," Sam said. He pointed up at the sun, which was almost directly overhead. "It'll be noon before long. They'll be opening the dam."

Robert gave orders: "Everyone grab a life jacket. Miss Foster, you sit in the front of the boat. Belinda and Andrew next. I'll work one of the oars, and Sam can work the other."

Everyone squeezed into the rowboat.

"What about the chocolates?" Miss Foster asked. "Shall I open the bag and scatter them in the lake?"

"No, I'll tie the bag to this piece of fishing line," Belinda said. "We'll drag it beside the boat."

"We'll go fishing for Alice!" said Andrew.

"And what should I do?" Miss Foster asked.

"Think about Alice as hard as you can," Robert said, sticking his oar in the water.

"Try to let her know we're coming to help her," added Sam.

Chapter Twelve

Slowly and carefully, Robert and Sam rowed out onto Spirit Lake.

Belinda dropped in her fishing line baited with chocolate.

Up close, the water looked even darker and spookier than before. And dirtier. Every time Robert and Sam dipped the oars into it, they brought up clumps of smelly water weeds.

"Yuck!" Andrew said. "Poor Alice must be slimed."

Belinda noticed that Miss Foster was wearing the silver compass on her dress. Her eyes were closed tightly. She was sending a message to her sister.

Belinda glanced at Sam. He leaned

his head to one side, listening hard. . . .

"Anything on the radar?" Belinda whispered to him.

"No . . . wait . . . *yes!*" Sam replied suddenly. "Let's turn the boat toward the middle of the lake," he said to Robert.

As they rowed, Sam tilted his head one way and then the other.

"The buzzing's getting louder . . ." he said. "Turn more to the left . . . more. . . ."

"Hey, look at those bubbles!" Andrew said.

In front of the rowboat, a mountain of bubbles boiled up from deep in the lake.

Belinda felt a fierce tug on the fishing line.

"Wow—something's really pulling on the chocolate!" she said.

"My radar's buzzing like a chain saw!" said Sam.

Miss Foster opened her eyes.

"Alice? Is that you, Alice?" Miss Foster cried. She leaned forward in the boat, staring down into the water.

Then they all heard Alice's bell.

And for a split second, they saw Alice herself!

She flew out of the water like a bright, white fish. She twisted in the air and landed in the boat beside Miss Foster.

Suddenly a huge wave broke over the side of the rowboat, drenching everyone. A lumpy human form burst out of the center of the wave.

It wasn't covered with mud anymore. It was wrapped in slimy, smelly lake weeds!

It was Gridley Pratt's ghost!

"Aaaaah!" the kids screamed.

Gridley grabbed the edge of the old rowboat. He shook it like a rag!

Miss Foster almost toppled into the water.

Belinda grabbed her around the waist. They tumbled to the bottom of the boat.

Robert lost his oar.

Andrew was crying.

Gridley was giggling, that gruesome, crazy giggling Belinda had heard the night before.

"He wants Alice!" Sam shouted.

"He wants *all* of us!" Belinda yelled.

"YOU CAN'T HAVE ALICE OR ANYONE ELSE!" boomed a very stern voice.

It was Miss Foster!

She struggled to her knees to face the horrible, smelly green creature that was Gridley's ghost.

"I know you, Gridley Pratt!" Miss Foster yelled right at him. *"You've always been a troublemaker and a bully!"*

The ghost was so surprised that he let go of the rowboat.

"You belong in the slime at the bottom of the lake!" shouted Miss Foster. *"Go back where you came from!"*

Suddenly, the boat rocked a little. It began to move away from Gridley, toward the shore of the lake.

"Something's pushing us . . ." said Belinda.

"It's the water flowing in from upriver!" Robert shouted.

Andrew stopped crying. "Yay!" he said. "It's noon. Gridley, you're toast!"

The boat started moving faster.

Gridley's head bobbed like a float, green slimy weeds swirling around it. As the Black Cat Club watched, he sank beneath the dark waters of Spirit Lake.

"The lake will be too deep for Gridley to bother us ever again," said Andrew.

"Just as long as it rains," Robert said, giving his knuckles a final crack.

"Miss Foster, that was incredible!" said Belinda. "You absolutely blew Gridley away!"

"Thank you," said Miss Foster. "I used to teach fourth grade. I just used my best schoolteacher tone."

The kids couldn't see Alice. But they could hear her.

Her bell was ringing louder and

louder. The air all around them smelled like chocolate.

"Miss Foster," said Belinda, "meet your sister Alice!"

Don't miss:
The Black Cat Club #5
The Revenge of the Pirate Ghost

"Summer's almost over," Sam Quirk said with a sigh.

It was the middle of a hot afternoon.

Sam was sitting on the wooden bench outside Snowflake Ice Cream, licking the drips off the side of a chocolate-chocolate-chip sugar cone.

"Next week we'll be in fourth grade," said Belinda Marks.

Belinda was also sitting on the bench, along with her little brother, Andrew. They were eating double-dip sugar cones too.

"But there's still time for the Black Cat Club to find another ghost," Sam said to them. "Maybe even two or three."

Sam had dreamed up the Black Cat

Club at the beginning of the summer to do just that: hunt down any ghosts that might be hanging around Maplewood.

The club had started out with four members: Sam, and Belinda and Andrew, who were his next-door neighbors on Mill Lane; and Robert Sullivan, who lived across the street from them.

"A ghost-hunting club?" Robert had said. "That's a totally dumb idea! I don't believe in ghosts."

Sam figured Robert was just mad because he hadn't thought of forming a club himself.

Whatever the reason, Robert was all wrong about ghosts.

A couple of days later, the Black Cat Club had discovered Alice Foster at the Maplewood library. Alice was *definitely* a ghost. . . .

Sam wondered where Alice was today. He'd ordered the chocolate-chocolate-chip cone in her honor.

But Sam's ears weren't even humming.

"Have you seen Alice?" he asked Andrew.

Andrew shook his head. "Maybe she's having fun with Robert," he said, grinning.

Andrew was joking. They all knew that just *thinking* about Alice made Robert crack his knuckles. He was really jumpy about her.

"Where *is* Robert?" Belinda asked. "He was supposed to be here at two o'clock."

"He's probably with Neal," Sam said, rolling his eyes.

Neal was Robert's thirteen-year-old cousin. He and his family were visiting from the city. Neal was a know-it-all who looked down on Robert and his friends because they were younger.

"I'll bet Robert is trying to ditch him right now," Sam said. . . .

Sam was right.

Robert was hanging out in his room, hoping Neal would get bored enough to leave.

Then Robert could go and meet Sam, Belinda, and Andrew at Snowflake Ice Cream.

But Neal was sprawled across Robert's bed, reading a comic book. He had blond hair, very big ears, and a bored expression on his face.

"So, what are you little guys up to this afternoon?" Neal asked Robert, leafing through the comic.

Like thirteen was so grown-up!

"Nothing much," Robert said. "Having a club meeting. Kid stuff," he mumbled, hoping Neal wasn't listening.

But Neal said, "What club?"

"The Black Cat Club," Robert said.

Neal closed the comic book. "'The Black Cat Club'? That sounds really *spooooky,*" he teased, rolling his eyes.

Neal thought he was *so* cool.

"What does the Black Cat Club do? Sit around telling *spooooooky* ghost stories?" Neal said. He added, "I thought you hated ghost stories!"

"Well, I grew up," said Robert, cracking his knuckles.

"Oh, yeah?" Neal said. "So those stories I used to tell you about Cousin Jedediah don't scare you anymore, huh?"

"No," said Robert nervously, thinking back.

When Robert was a little kid, Neal used to try to scare him with creepy stories about an evil relative of theirs named Jedediah Sullivan.

Jedediah Sullivan, Neal said, was a fearsome pirate. About a hundred and fifty years ago, Jedediah and his men sailed up and down the coast in a ship called *The Fury*.

The pirates robbed other ships and held passengers for ransom. If the passengers' families didn't pay up quickly enough, Jedediah would threaten to cut off the hostages' ears or noses. Sometimes he did it, too.

The law didn't catch up with Jedediah until he'd retired from pirating, changed his name, and moved back to Maplewood. He built a house somewhere on the north side of town, near the lake.

But there was a big bounty on Jedediah's head. Anyone who turned him in would be rewarded with one hundred pieces of gold.

So somebody in the Sullivan family told the sheriff where Jedediah was.

The sheriff and his deputies sneaked up on Jedediah at his new house. They grabbed the old pirate and hanged him from a tree in his own front yard.

At this point in the story, Neal would make gagging and choking noises, like Jedediah Sullivan with the noose tightening slo-o-owly around his neck.

Years later, Robert could still hear those horrible strangling sounds.

"You know what Jedediah said just as they put the noose around his neck?" Neal had asked. "He said that one day he'd return and get his revenge. There's a legend about it that says Jedediah has one chance to come back and even the score with his family."

Then Neal would shake his finger in Robert's face. "And it's *all true*! Great-Uncle Wesley told me. So watch out— when you least expect it, Cousin Jedediah might sneak up on you and cut your nose off!"

Robert shivered at the memory. He stared at Neal. "Those were stories you made up to scare me," he said.

Neal just smirked at him.

Robert gulped. He didn't believe in the curse of Jedediah Sullivan. *Did he?*